Elemental Heart

A Dance of Love and Power

(The Elemental Chronicles Series)
Book 1

Bea Welliver

This is a work of fiction. Names, characters, places, and incidents either are the product of the author's imagination or are used fictitiously. Any resemblance to actual persons, living or dead, events, or locales is entirely coincidental.

Table of Contents

Chapter 1: Unveiling of Powers

Our tale begins in the small, unassuming village of Faelore, nestled between sprawling mountains and a crystal-clear lake. Life is tranquil here, untouched by the worries of the world beyond. In this pastoral haven lives Elara, an eighteen-year-old girl with fiery red hair, expressive emerald eyes, and a spirit that sings of uncharted adventures.

Like other villagers, Elara lives a simple life, aiding her mother in their small apothecary shop. Her days are spent picking herbs and brewing remedies for the locals. Despite the humble and monotonous life, Elara finds herself drawn to the mysterious world of herbs, captivated by their latent energies. Yet, a part of her yearns for something more, something beyond the borders of Faelore.

One day, as Elara prepares a potion for an ailing villager, something extraordinary happens. A usual concoction requires a careful balance of herbs, but today, she absentmindedly adds an unusual ingredient - a dried petal of a Starfall Blossom, a flower rumored to have fallen from the stars. Unbeknownst to Elara, the Starfall Blossom carries a latent magical essence.

As she stirs the potion, it suddenly glows an ethereal blue, lighting up the entire room. Startled, Elara tries to pull her hand away, but it's as if an unseen force has a hold of her, guiding her actions. She watches in wide-eyed astonishment as the winds outside pick up, swirling in a vortex, and the room's temperature fluctuates wildly.

Suddenly, the water from a bucket in the corner rises and shapes itself into a water orb, hovering in the air. The fire from the hearth rages and dances, seeming to respond to her heartbeat. The soil from the plant pots lifts, circling the room like a miniature sandstorm, while the metal tools begin to tremble, as if trying to break free from an invisible magnetic field.

Fear and awe war within Elara as she witnesses the unbelievable spectacle – the elements are responding to her, bending to her will. She feels a deep connection, a sense of raw, unbridled power pulsing within her. As quickly as it starts, the phenomenon ends, the elements settling back down, leaving Elara panting and the room in disarray.

The realization dawns on Elara: she isn't just an ordinary girl from a small village. She's a sorceress with the power to control the elements.

She spends the rest of the day in a daze, her mind teeming with questions. Why her? How did this happen? Is she a danger to her family, her village? The world as she knows it has been flipped upside down, and Elara stands on the precipice of a life that is about to become anything but ordinary. Little does she know, her journey has only just begun. And with great power, as they say, comes great responsibility – and a dash of romance that would make any mortal's heart race.

Chapter 2: The Elemental Affair

Following her encounter with her newfound power, Elara is left overwhelmed. She spends the night wrestling with her thoughts, anxiously pondering the implications of her abilities. As dawn breaks, she finds herself devoid of sleep, but filled with a sense of determination.

Elara decides to understand her powers better, thinking that perhaps if she learns to control them, she can ensure that no harm befalls those around her. With this in mind, she ventures into the secluded heart of the nearby forest, a place where the villagers seldom tread, away from prying eyes.

Here, amidst the quiet rustling of leaves and the gentle chirping of birds, she begins to experiment. Tentatively at first, she attempts to connect with the elements, just as she had done unconsciously in the apothecary shop. She reaches out with her senses, trying to feel the energy of the earth beneath her, the air around her, the small rivulet nearby, and the warmth of the sun above.

To her surprise, the elements respond. The earth vibrates softly beneath her feet, the water in the rivulet stirs, the breeze plays with her hair, and she feels an odd kinship with the flickering rays of the sun. But controlling them is another matter. Every time she tries to command an element, it reacts too strongly, escalating quickly and becoming chaotic.

She accidentally causes the rivulet to overflow, sends gusts of wind whipping violently through the trees, and the earth cracks and rumbles beneath her. Each incident only causes her to panic more, escalating her powers out of control.

Exhausted and frustrated, Elara slumps down against a tree, despair beginning to seep into her thoughts. It's then she hears it - a rustling behind her. Spinning around, she comes face to face with a direwolf, its teeth bared and eyes aflame. Fear courses through her, causing the elements to react in a wild, chaotic display.

As the direwolf lunges, Elara instinctively throws up her hand, and a wall of fire springs to life between her and the beast. The direwolf retreats with a whimper, frightened by the sudden flame. The fire, unlike the previous chaotic reactions, responds smoothly to her command, dancing and swaying as she wills it, as though a part of her own being.

Elara is left standing, arm outstretched, the firelight reflecting in her wide eyes. This marks the first time she has successfully controlled an element. With renewed confidence and hope, she realizes that while her journey to understanding her powers may be difficult, it isn't impossible.

But as the sun dips below the horizon and she makes her way home, she can't shake the feeling of being watched. Unbeknownst to her, the incident with the direwolf did not go unnoticed. From the shadows, a figure - a man clad in armor, bearing the crest of the local lord - has been observing her, his eyes reflecting surprise and a hint of worry. This man, the knight who is to become her protector, will soon play a significant role in Elara's life, bringing with him not just protection, but a forbidden love.

Chapter 3: The Knight's Vow

In the dead of night, the armored figure gallops back towards the imposing castle that overlooks the village of Faelore. This man is Sir Alden, a highly respected knight renowned for his bravery and valor, now burdened with an unforeseen revelation - the existence of a sorceress within their peaceful village.

Upon reaching the castle, he seeks an audience with the local lord, an old, wise man known as Lord Caelius. Caelius is stunned by the news of a sorceress in Faelore. He knows the magical world too well, for he was once part of it before renouncing it for a simpler life. Aware of the dangers that lie ahead, Caelius assigns Sir Alden to be Elara's protector, unbeknownst to her, to keep her safe from those who might exploit her powers.

Reluctantly, Alden accepts his new role. His knightly vows demand his loyalty to his lord, but he's uncertain about this new task. He's fought fearsome beasts and formidable warriors, but protecting a sorceress? This was uncharted territory.

The next day, Alden finds himself nervously heading to Elara's humble home under the guise of purchasing a remedy for an ailing comrade. As he enters the apothecary, he's taken aback by the sight of Elara. He had seen her from afar, but up close, her radiance is different, vibrant. Her fiery red hair dances in the sunlight pouring in through the windows, and her emerald eyes seem to hold a world of their own. A peculiar energy surrounds her, one that he finds oddly comforting and alluring.

Elara is equally surprised by the knight's visit. She had seen Sir Alden during local festivities and from the occasional visits he made to the village. The villagers held him in high regard, and the younger girls often swooned over the tall, brooding knight with striking blue eyes. Elara had always admired him from afar but never imagined meeting him up close.

As Elara prepares the remedy, the two engage in light conversation. Elara finds herself drawn to the knight, surprised by the kindness and understanding behind his stern facade. Alden, in turn, finds Elara's passion for her work and the spark in her eyes enchanting. An unspoken connection sparks between the two, a chemistry that they both quietly acknowledge but choose to ignore.

As Alden leaves the apothecary, he looks back to find Elara waving him goodbye, a soft smile playing on her lips. He turns away, a peculiar warmth spreading through his heart. He realizes then that his duty may prove to be more complicated than he'd expected. He's been tasked with protecting Elara, but will he be able to protect his own heart in the process?

Thus begins Alden's silent vigil, a task marked by his duty as a knight, and a burgeoning emotion he's yet to comprehend. As he steps into this new role, he makes a silent vow - he will keep Elara safe, not just out of duty, but because he desires to. Little does he know, this vow will entangle him in a web of magic, power, and forbidden love.

Chapter 4: Crossing Realms

While Elara begins to build an unexpected bond with the knight Alden, there's a disturbance in a realm far removed from the mundane world of Faelore. The Dark Kingdom, home to an ancient race of magic wielders, sits at the edge of reality, separated from the mortal realm by a magical barrier.

Here reigns Prince Darius, a figure of power and fear, known for his ruthlessly cunning nature and an allure that's almost as dangerous. With his jet-black hair, piercing purple eyes, and a brooding persona, he is a prince wrapped in enigma and feared by many.

The Dark Kingdom has long been searching for a way to increase its power. The King's seeress has a vision of a girl with the power of the elements - a power that, if harnessed, could change the fortunes of their kingdom.

Darius, intrigued by the prophecy and bored by the monotony of his dark realm, decides to cross over into the mortal world. Despite the rules that prohibit interaction between their worlds, the promise of power and the image of the fiery-haired girl with emerald eyes compels him.

Using a forbidden incantation, Darius manages to tear a portal into the mortal realm, stepping out into the vibrant greens of Faelore, a stark contrast to the eternal twilight of his dark kingdom. The moment he steps into the mortal realm, he can feel a powerful energy that he's never felt before - the pure, uncontrolled energy of an elemental sorceress. The energy signature matches that of the girl from the seeress's vision. Elara.

For the first time in centuries, Darius feels a thrill of anticipation. The girl may not know it yet, but her life is about to become inextricably intertwined with his. He fades into the shadows, planning his next move, vowing to find this elemental sorceress and unlock the power that could save his realm.

Little does he know that his appearance in the mortal realm hasn't gone unnoticed. Elara, sensitive to the ebb and flow of magic, feels a sudden surge in power. The world around her seems to quiver momentarily, like a plucked string. She feels an unexplainable sense of foreboding, a feeling that something, or someone, has disrupted the balance of her world.

Unbeknownst to both, their paths are set to cross in a dance of power, magic, and a forbidden love that threatens to consume everything in its path.

Chapter 5: Dark Attraction

A week has passed since Darius made his way into the mortal realm. He has been observing Elara from afar, intrigued by her raw, untrained power. He's fascinated by her simple yet fulfilling life - her bond with her family, her dedication to her work, and her undying spirit to understand and control her powers.

While Darius is busy studying Elara, she can't shake off the unsettling feeling of being watched. She feels a pull, an unusual energy that she can't quite place. Her powers are growing stronger, and with it, her sensitivity to otherworldly forces. However, she keeps these feelings to herself, not wanting to alarm her family or Sir Alden.

One evening, as Elara returns from her secret practice in the forest, she takes a detour through the meadows. The sun has just set, and under the soft twilight, the field looks enchanting. Suddenly, she senses a strong pulse of energy. Turning around, she finds herself standing a few feet away from a tall, shadowy figure. The figure steps into the moonlight, revealing himself to be a man of extraordinary beauty. His jet-black hair, piercing purple eyes, and the strange yet alluring aura take Elara's breath away. This man is Darius, the dark prince.

Darius had not planned this encounter, but once he saw Elara alone, curiosity got the better of him. He introduces himself as a wanderer, omitting his true identity and his realm. Elara, though taken aback, feels an odd sense of familiarity towards him. Their conversation flows easily. Darius's charm, coupled with his knowledge of magic and the world beyond Faelore, has Elara hanging onto his every word.

The more Darius learns about Elara, the more he finds himself drawn to her. He's captivated by her strength, her passion for her newfound powers, and her love for her family and village. Despite his initial intentions, Darius finds himself entangled in the web of Elara's charm. The attraction he feels towards her is strong and unfamiliar. He, who has always been the pursuer, now finds himself being drawn in.

For Elara, her attraction to the dark stranger is equally unsettling. She can't deny the chemistry between them, but her thoughts keep straying to Sir Alden. His steady presence in her life and his silent, comforting support have carved a place in her heart. Torn between her attraction to the dark, mysterious stranger and her growing feelings for Alden, Elara finds herself in the middle of a romantic chaos she never saw coming.

As Darius parts from her with a promise to meet again, Elara watches his retreating figure with mixed emotions. Unknown to her, this unplanned meeting will only serve to complicate her life further, adding fuel to the already complicated triangle of power, love, and destiny.

Chapter 6: Training Begins

With the emergence of this mysterious stranger, Sir Alden, who has been observing from a distance, feels an immediate sense of alarm. He recognizes an underlying danger in the stranger's interactions with Elara. He decides it's time to step in and ensure her safety.

Alden, carrying the weight of his silent oath, approaches Elara one morning, expressing his wish to help her train and control her powers. Elara is taken aback initially but agrees upon understanding his sincere concern for her. He explains that Lord Caelius has knowledge of magic from his past and has agreed to guide them through the process.

Thus, the training begins. Under Caelius's instructions, Alden starts with helping Elara focus her energy. The training is not just physical but also mental and spiritual. Elara is taught to meditate, to center herself, to reach out to the elements with not just her powers but also her emotions.

Alden proves to be a patient teacher, correcting her, encouraging her, and most importantly, supporting her. He's by her side when the training becomes too overwhelming, offering solace with his comforting presence. This brings them even closer, their bond strengthening with each passing day.

Elara's progress surprises them all. She has an inherent connection with fire and water, and under Alden's training, she learns to control them, using her will to command them. Her affinity with earth and air needs more work, but she's not discouraged. She's determined to master all elements, driven by an insatiable thirst for knowledge and a desire to protect those she loves.

While Elara trains with Alden, she still meets with Darius, her mysterious stranger, whenever she can. Darius is always willing to share his knowledge about magic, providing her with a different perspective. His words often help her during her training with Alden, a fact she keeps to herself. She finds herself drawn into this complicated relationship, unable to resist the allure of the dark prince and the comfort of her steadfast knight.

As the days pass, Elara grows stronger, more in control of her powers. Her life becomes a whirlwind of training sessions, quiet moments with Alden, and secretive meetings with Darius. She's standing on the precipice of a complicated love triangle and a hidden war for power she's yet to comprehend fully. She's blissfully unaware that every step she takes is pulling her deeper into a world of magic, politics, and a love that could shake the very foundations of her world.

Chapter 7: The King's Warning

While Elara's life in the mortal realm is entwined with training and complex emotions, the dark realm is in unrest. King Orion, Darius's father, is growing increasingly impatient. He's aware of Darius's frequent visits to the mortal realm and his growing affection for the sorceress.

Despite his son's entanglement, the King focuses on the prophecy and the power it promises. He summons Darius to the throne room, an imposing space with obsidian walls and an ever-burning magical fire that dances with hues of deep purple and black. The King sits on his massive throne made from dark crystals, exuding an aura of power and authority.

Darius enters, his face betraying nothing of his feelings for Elara or his conflict regarding his father's plans. The King, with his deep, commanding voice, warns Darius about the dangers of developing feelings for the sorceress. He reminds him of their dwindling power and the prophecy that could be their salvation.

He warns Darius of the consequences of straying from their path. Their kingdom is hanging by a thread, and the sorceress's powers are the only thing that can tip the balance in their favor. If Darius fails or allows his personal feelings to obstruct their goal, the entire kingdom could crumble into oblivion.

Darius is torn. He understands his duty towards his people, his kingdom. But his meetings with Elara have stirred feelings he hadn't anticipated. He's drawn to her spirit, her energy, and the spark that seems to connect them. Yet, he knows his father speaks the truth.

Torn between his duty and his growing love for Elara, Darius makes a promise to his father. He assures the King that he will bring Elara to their realm, promising to fulfill the prophecy. However, he remains silent about his emotions, vowing to himself to protect Elara, even if it means going against his own kingdom.

Unaware of the promise Darius has made, Elara continues her training. She grows more powerful with each passing day, unknowingly drawing the attention of forces far beyond her comprehension. As the shadow of the Dark Kingdom looms closer, the ties of love, friendship, and duty get more tangled, ready to set the stage for a tale of epic proportions.

Chapter 8: Hidden Hearts

As the days pass, Elara finds herself deeply immersed in her training with Alden and her secret meetings with Darius. Despite her initial resistance, she finds herself attracted to both of them, each in their unique way.

Alden, with his patience and strength, provides her with a sense of security she didn't know she craved. She respects his dedication to his duties, and his unwavering support during her training sessions has endeared him to her. There is a warmth in their companionship, a comfortable silence, an unspoken bond that Elara can't ignore. She finds herself caring for him, worrying about him, and wanting to be around him.

Darius, on the other hand, brings a thrill she hadn't known before. His knowledge about magic, the world beyond Faelore, and his charm have a magnetic pull. Despite his mysterious aura, she finds herself trusting him, sharing her fears and dreams. Their conversations often last for hours under the moonlit sky, strengthening their connection.

However, Elara also senses a hidden pain in Darius, a loneliness she wishes she could ease. She's intrigued by him and the more time they spend together, the more her feelings for him grow. His words, his presence, and the intensity in his eyes stir feelings in her she didn't know she was capable of.

Meanwhile, Darius finds himself caught in his promise to his father and his growing affection for Elara. He continues to meet Elara, torn between his duty and his heart. Every smile, every word, every shared moment only serves to deepen his feelings for her.

On the other hand, Alden is fighting his own battle. He's acutely aware of Elara's growing powers, and he can't ignore the pull he feels towards her. His vow to protect her is more than just a duty now. Yet, he keeps his feelings hidden, fearing it might cloud his judgment or, worse, put Elara in danger.

In the midst of her training and her tangled emotions, Elara's life takes on a rhythm of its own. Her days are filled with elemental magic, her evenings with the mysterious Darius, and her quiet moments with the steadfast Alden. As she explores her powers and her feelings for the two men, she remains oblivious to the storm that's brewing, ready to shatter the peace of her world.

Chapter 9: Betrayal's Shadow

Just as Elara feels that she is beginning to find some semblance of balance in her life, the first sign of the storm brewing in the horizon reaches her. A messenger arrives at Faelore bearing news of a neighboring kingdom being attacked by an unknown force of immense power. This kingdom, just like Faelore, had been peaceful and had never participated in the ongoing power struggles.

Elara immediately senses the work of dark magic behind this. The reality of the danger her world is in becomes more concrete. She fears that this unknown force might find its way to Faelore next, and she realizes she needs to master her powers quickly, not just for her but also for her people.

In the meantime, Darius is battling his inner turmoil. He has learned about the attack and knows that it's the doing of his father. He struggles to reconcile the man he knows with the King who would harm innocents in his quest for power. He's torn between his loyalty towards his kingdom and his love for Elara.

Elara, unaware of Darius's predicament, seeks him out, hoping that he can shed some light on the situation. But Darius, desperate to protect Elara, hides the truth from her. He assures her that he will find out more about the attack and that she should focus on her training.

Feeling helpless, Elara confides in Alden, sharing her fears and worries. Alden, who has been noticing Darius's odd behavior, is on high alert. He feels the stirrings of doubt and suspects that Darius might have more information than he's letting on.

One evening, as Alden is on his routine patrol, he stumbles upon Elara and Darius during one of their secret meetings. He sees them engaged in a close conversation, their body language indicating a level of intimacy that fuels a spark of jealousy and suspicion.

Deciding to confront Darius, Alden reveals his presence. Darius, caught off guard, struggles to explain his relationship with Elara to Alden. Elara is shocked and hurt by Alden's accusations and Darius's inability to defend himself convincingly.

Alden warns Darius to stay away from Elara, vowing to uncover his secrets. Darius, wracked with guilt and fear, can do little but watch as Alden storms away, leaving Elara in tears. This incident casts a dark shadow over Elara and Darius's relationship, a shadow of betrayal that threatens to consume them and alter the course of their destiny.

Chapter 10: Elemental Mastery

The aftermath of the confrontation sees Elara, Alden, and Darius entangled in a web of mixed emotions, suspicion, and looming threats. Elara feels betrayed by Darius, not for keeping their meetings a secret but for hiding the truth about the attack. She's equally upset with Alden for not trusting her. She finds herself isolated and heartbroken.

Alden, on the other hand, is consumed by a sense of guilt for hurting Elara and an anger towards Darius, whom he sees as a threat to Elara. He seeks out Lord Caelius, expressing his suspicions about Darius. Caelius, a wise old man, counsels patience and understanding, reminding Alden that all may not be as it seems.

Despite her emotional turmoil, Elara knows she needs to focus on her training more than ever. The fear for her kingdom and her people outweighs her personal grievances. She throws herself into her training with a newfound determination, channeling her anger, confusion, and fear into her connection with the elements.

The intense emotional state serves as a catalyst, pushing her connection with the elements to a new level. She starts to master not just fire and water but also earth and air. Her control over the elements becomes more nuanced, almost intuitive, a part of her as natural as breathing.

Alden, despite his conflicting emotions, continues to support Elara in her training. He recognizes the progress she's making and can't help but admire her resilience. They work together, their bond of friendship and shared responsibility managing to withstand the test of recent events.

While Elara grows stronger, Darius wrestles with his guilt and fear. He's torn between his duty to his father and his love for Elara. The King grows impatient, pressing Darius for results. Darius promises to bring Elara to the Dark Kingdom soon, buying time while he figures out a way to protect Elara without betraying his father.

As Elara nears her elemental mastery, the stakes get higher. The balance of power is about to shift, and hearts are about to be tested. Elara, Alden, and Darius are on the brink of decisions and revelations that will alter their lives forever. The story of love, betrayal, and magic gets more complicated, setting the stage for an epic showdown between the forces of light and darkness.

Chapter 11: The Dark Prince's Secret

Haunted by his promise to the King and the mounting tension with Elara and Alden, Darius is under immense pressure. He realizes that it's time to unveil the truth and deal with the consequences. However, he fears the revelation might ruin his budding relationship with Elara and put her in danger.

Unable to bear the weight of his secrets any longer, Darius seeks out Elara. He finds her at the training grounds, her face etched with concentration as she controls the wind around her. Watching her, Darius feels a surge of affection and respect. He knows revealing his identity could cost him everything, but he owes her the truth.

Bracing himself, Darius approaches Elara. Seeing him, she initially stiffens, still hurt from the events of the previous days.

However, the seriousness in his eyes prompts her to listen. In a low, regretful voice, Darius tells her everything. He unveils his identity as the dark prince, explains the prophecy, his father's ambition, and the looming danger.

Elara is stunned. The revelation hits her hard, but she's more hurt by Darius's lack of trust than his true identity. Darius apologizes, insisting that his feelings for her are genuine and that he only wanted to protect her. His vulnerability touches Elara, but she's overwhelmed and asks him to leave.

Once alone, Elara struggles to process the revelation. Her mind races, torn between a sense of betrayal and concern for Darius. She's shocked to know the man she's been developing feelings for is the prince of the realm she fears.

Meanwhile, Alden stumbles upon a distraught Elara. Upon asking, Elara discloses Darius's secret. Alden is enraged but also worried for Elara. He promises to protect her, no matter what. Their shared worry for Faelore and their unresolved feelings for each other bring them closer.

The revelation of the dark prince's secret changes the dynamics between Elara, Darius, and Alden. Trust is shattered, alliances are tested, and hearts are broken. However, amid the chaos, the three of them also find an unyielding resolve to protect what they hold dear. Unbeknownst to them, their actions are setting the course for a struggle that could either save or doom their worlds.

Chapter 12: Knight's Dilemma

After the revelation of Darius's true identity, Alden finds himself in a quandary. As a knight, his duty is to protect Elara and Faelore from any harm. However, with Darius's revelation, Alden realizes the danger is far closer and more significant than he initially thought. He grapples with his emerging feelings for Elara and his responsibility as a knight.

His first impulse is to inform the King about Darius, but he knows it could put Elara in immediate danger. He decides to confront Darius first. He meets Darius at the border of Faelore, challenging him and accusing him of deceit. Darius accepts the accusations but insists that he never meant to harm Elara. He proposes a temporary truce for Elara's sake, which Alden reluctantly accepts.

Elara, unaware of the confrontation between Alden and Darius, is fighting her own battles. She's hurt and confused. Despite her anger at Darius, she can't ignore the connection she felt with him. At the same time, her bond with Alden grows stronger as they navigate through the crisis together.

Alden, in his attempt to protect Elara, finds himself growing closer to her. He admires her resilience and her dedication to her training despite the emotional turmoil. They spend long hours practicing, strategizing, and sharing quiet moments. These moments, laden with unspoken feelings and a deep sense of camaraderie, confuse Alden further.

His role as a knight demands that he stay focused on the impending danger and not get swayed by his emotions. However, his heart yearns for the comfort and connection he finds with Elara. Torn between duty and desire, Alden finds himself in a dilemma.

Meanwhile, Darius is dealing with his own troubles. His father grows more impatient, and the kingdom's unrest increases. The gap between his duty as a prince and his desires as a man widens, putting Darius under immense pressure.

As Alden, Elara, and Darius navigate their dilemmas, their decisions and actions continue to weave a complex web of love, duty, and betrayal. With each passing day, the impending clash between the realms grows nearer, threatening to disrupt the delicate balance they are trying to maintain.

Chapter 13: The Sorceress Revealed

Elara's days pass in a haze of training, planning, and emotional turmoil. Her heart aches for Darius, but Alden's steady presence and support soothe her. Meanwhile, her elemental mastery grows, surprising even Alden with her rapid progress. She can now not only control the elements individually, but also combine them to create powerful effects.

Their relative peace shatters when Faelore receives a delegation from the Dark Kingdom, led by none other than King Zephyros himself. He announces his intention to form an alliance through marriage, proposing Darius as a suitor for Princess Elara, whom he believes is the prophesied sorceress.

A wave of shock sweeps over the court. Elara, standing beside King Adair, feels a cold dread. She looks at Darius, who appears equally shocked. King Adair, however, hides his surprise well. He cordially thanks King Zephyros for his proposal but asks for time to discuss the matter with his council and his daughter.

King Zephyros agrees, leaving behind an air of tension as he withdraws. The revelation shakes the court, and whispers of the sorceress amongst them start to circulate. Elara, with Alden by her side, finds herself the center of curious, fearful, and awestruck gazes.

Elara retreats to her chambers, her mind whirling. Alden accompanies her, offering silent support. They both know they have little time to make a decision. Alden promises Elara he will stand by her, whatever the choice.

Meanwhile, Darius confronts his father, angry about the unexpected proposal. King Zephyros coolly reveals that he knew about Darius's secret meetings with Elara and his son's growing affection for her. The King believes this marriage will not only fulfill the prophecy but also tie Darius's loyalties firmly to the Dark Kingdom.

As the news of the proposed alliance spreads through Faelore, Elara's identity as the sorceress becomes the talk of the kingdom. Her world, once again, is thrown into chaos. However, the revelation also solidifies her resolve to protect her kingdom, her people, and herself. The course is set for battles, both of the heart and the kingdoms.

Chapter 14: Love's Sacrifice

The proposal from the Dark Kingdom sends shockwaves through Faelore. The court is divided, with some believing the alliance could protect them, while others fear it could be their downfall. Elara is at the center of it all, her secret identity as the sorceress now a common knowledge.

Despite the pressure, Elara remains steadfast. She spends hours in council with her father and his advisors, discussing the potential repercussions of the alliance. She knows that the decision could make or break her kingdom.

Alden is by her side through it all, his support unwavering. He struggles with his feelings for Elara and the thought of losing her to Darius. However, he suppresses his emotions, focusing on the bigger picture - the safety of Faelore and Elara.

In the Dark Kingdom, Darius is grappling with his father's revelation. His heart yearns for Elara, but he's aware of the consequences if he goes against his father's wishes. The turmoil within him is tearing him apart.

In the midst of the chaos, Elara seeks solace in her training. She channels her stress, fear, and anger into her elemental control, pushing her limits. Her powers grow, now commanding not only the elements but also the energy that binds them.

One day, after a particularly grueling training session, Alden confesses his feelings for Elara. It's a quiet, heartfelt admission, full of longing and sadness. Elara is taken aback. She values their friendship and respects Alden, but she's unsure about her feelings. Alden, understanding her confusion, assures her that he doesn't expect anything and will continue to support her no matter what.

The proposal deadline is approaching. Elara, after much deliberation, decides to accept the proposal. She sees it as a necessary sacrifice for the safety of her kingdom. Her decision breaks Alden's heart, but he respects her choice, vowing to protect her even if it means watching her marry another.

In the Dark Kingdom, Darius receives the news with mixed feelings. He's overjoyed that Elara accepted, but he's also afraid of the danger his father's ambition poses to her. He makes a silent promise to protect Elara, even if it means going against his father.

As Elara makes her sacrifice, the lines between love, duty, and sacrifice blur. The stage is set for a royal wedding, alliances are tested, and hearts are on the line. Little do they know, the real battle is just around the corner.

Chapter 15: Prince vs. Knight

The news of Elara's acceptance of the marriage proposal sends a ripple of surprise, fear, and anticipation through both kingdoms. Preparations for the royal wedding begin in full swing in Faelore, the usually calm and serene kingdom now buzzing with activity.

Despite the impending nuptials, Elara doesn't halt her training. Her powers continue to grow, her connection with the elements becoming more profound. Amidst the wedding chaos, she finds solace and focus in her training. Alden, despite his broken heart, remains her unwavering pillar of support, assisting her in her training.

In the Dark Kingdom, Darius struggles with his own tumult of emotions. He's ecstatic about the upcoming wedding but deeply concerned about his father's ambitions. He knows he must stay vigilant to protect Elara. He begins to train harder, preparing himself for any potential threat.

Back in Faelore, the day of a grand feast before the wedding arrives. Nobility from both kingdoms gather, the atmosphere fraught with excitement, tension, and unspoken conflicts. Darius and Elara meet publicly for the first time since the proposal, their connection palpable yet strained. Alden, forced to watch the woman he loves with another, feels a surge of jealousy and resentment.

As the feast progresses, a friendly challenge is proposed - a traditional sword fight between the groom-to-be and a knight of the bride's kingdom. Darius and Alden find themselves pitted against each other, their personal conflicts now taking a physical form.

The duel is intense, showcasing Darius's dark, raw power against Alden's disciplined, honed skills. The onlookers watch with bated breath as the prince and the knight spar. The tension is palpable, with each parry and thrust mirroring their emotional battle. Despite their personal issues, their fight remains respectful and fair, a testament to their love for Elara.

The duel ends with no clear winner, but it establishes a newfound understanding and grudging respect between Darius and Alden. They both realize that their common goal is Elara's safety and happiness, regardless of their personal feelings.

As the night ends, Elara finds herself torn between her duty and her heart. She feels a pull towards Darius, but Alden's constant support and unspoken love weigh on her mind. With her wedding approaching and the kingdoms teetering on the edge of a great conflict, Elara finds herself in the eye of a storm, her decisions having far-reaching consequences.

Chapter 16: Battle of Elements

As the day of the wedding nears, tensions rise in both the Dark Kingdom and Faelore. The citizens of both realms are torn between the anticipation of a grand royal wedding and the fear of a prophecy looming overhead. Amidst all this, Elara, Darius, and Alden are caught up in their personal dilemmas.

On the eve of her wedding, Elara has a troubling dream. She sees herself standing alone amidst chaos and destruction, her elemental powers uncontrollable and wild. She wakes up in a cold sweat, the image of the dream imprinted on her mind.

As the day dawns, the wedding preparations reach their peak. Elara is dressed in the traditional wedding attire of Faelore, looking every bit the radiant princess she is.

Despite her external calm, she battles an internal storm of uncertainty and fear.

During the ceremony, Elara's nightmare becomes a reality. A force, dark and foreboding, attacks the kingdom. It is the work of rogue sorcerers from the Dark Kingdom, defying King Zephyros's orders in their belief that the prophecy will bring doom upon their kingdom.

In the ensuing chaos, Elara's elemental powers emerge full force. Her fear and protective instincts for her kingdom and people fuel her magic. She stands, a beacon amidst the chaos, her elements swirling around her.

Alden, despite his shock at the sudden attack, is quick to defend his princess and kingdom. He engages the invaders, his knightly prowess shining through. Darius, torn between his duty towards his kingdom and his love for Elara, eventually joins the fight against his rogue countrymen.

The battle is fierce, and Elara, Alden, and Darius find themselves in the heart of it. Elara, using her powers, repels the attackers. With Alden and Darius by her side, they form a formidable force.

As the battle intensifies, Elara channels her elements, creating a barrier around the kingdom. With one last surge of power, she manages to expel the rogue sorcerers, leaving them stunned and powerless outside the barrier.

Exhausted but victorious, Elara collapses into Alden's arms. Darius, looking on, realizes the extent of Elara's powers and the threat they may pose to his kingdom if provoked. The realization strikes a chord in him, filling him with fear and awe.

In the aftermath of the battle, Elara, Alden, and Darius have a new understanding of their roles, their powers, and the delicacy of their situation. The threat of another attack looms heavy, but for now, Faelore is safe, and the trio stands united.

Chapter 17: The Heart's Decision

After the sudden attack and the display of Elara's powerful magic, Faelore is in disarray. While the people are astounded by their princess's abilities, there's also a current of fear for what this means for their kingdom. Elara, recovering from the exertion of the battle, is kept away from the public eye to rest and recuperate.

Alden stays by her side, his protective instincts stronger than ever. He can't help but admire Elara's strength and courage. He sees her struggle with the weight of her powers and the impact of her decisions, and his heart aches for her.

Darius, on the other hand, finds himself conflicted. His love for Elara remains strong, but seeing her immense power has also brought fear. He worries about the future of his kingdom, and whether his love for Elara will put his people in danger. This internal struggle causes a rift between Darius and Elara, with Darius avoiding her to sort through his feelings.

In the aftermath of the battle, Elara spends her time reflecting. She ponders over her feelings for Darius and Alden. She acknowledges the strong connection she feels with Darius, but she's also deeply aware of Alden's unwavering support and love. She feels torn between the dark prince and the loyal knight.

One day, while she's resting, Alden comes to see her. He tells her that no matter her decision, he'll always be there for her. His sincerity and warmth bring tears to her eyes, and for the first time, she sees Alden not just as her protector, but as a man who truly loves her.

On the other hand, Darius finally gathers the courage to confront Elara. He confesses his fear and concern, making Elara see the reality of their situation. Despite the deep love they have for each other, they belong to different worlds that might soon be at odds.

After days of reflection and heartache, Elara finally makes a decision. She chooses Alden, the man who has been her constant support, her pillar of strength. She sees a future with him, a future where she can be not just a sorceress, but a woman in love.

Her decision brings relief to Alden and heartache to Darius. But Darius respects her choice and promises to uphold the alliance for the sake of their kingdoms. The heart's decision has been made, but it's just the beginning of their intertwined destinies.

Chapter 18: Ultimate Betrayal

Following her heart's decision, Elara experiences a sense of peace she hasn't felt in a long time. Her relationship with Alden blossoms, their bond growing stronger with each passing day. Despite the heartbreak, Darius remains true to his word, maintaining a courteous, if distant, relationship with Elara.

However, not everyone in the Dark Kingdom is pleased with the turn of events. There are those who still fear Elara's power and the prophecy associated with her. One such person is Darius's personal advisor, Malak, who had always held suspicions about the union between the Dark Prince and the Sorceress of Faelore.

Malak orchestrates a devious plan behind Darius's back. He sends a secret message to a group of rebel sorcerers within Faelore, informing them about a vulnerability in Elara's magical defenses. This information gives the rebel sorcerers an opportunity to attack Elara and strip her of her powers.

Darius, completely oblivious to Malak's betrayal, is horrified when he discovers the attack on Elara. He rushes to her aid, only to find her severely weakened. Alden, who was by Elara's side during the attack, is filled with anger and guilt for not being able to protect her.

Darius confronts Malak, who doesn't deny his actions, instead revealing his fear of Elara's power and the prophecy. He argues that he did it for the greater good of the Dark Kingdom. Darius, filled with rage and betrayal, banishes Malak from the kingdom.

Meanwhile, Alden stays by Elara's side as she fights to recover from the attack. The event brings them even closer, and Alden's protective and caring nature comforts Elara in her moment of vulnerability.

The betrayal shakes the alliance between Faelore and the Dark Kingdom. Trust is broken, and the fear of another attack is prevalent. Elara, despite her weakened state, vows to get stronger to protect her people. As the chapter ends, she must navigate through this ultimate betrayal, mend the shaky alliance, and reclaim her full powers.

Chapter 19: Battle for Love

In the aftermath of the ultimate betrayal, both Faelore and the Dark Kingdom are in a state of unease. Darius regrets the deceit that has occurred from his kingdom and worries about the impact on his alliance with Faelore. Meanwhile, Alden can't shake off the guilt of not being able to protect Elara from the attack.

Elara, despite her weakened state, doesn't lose her spirit. With Alden's support, she begins to rebuild her strength and regain control over her elements. The ordeal has only reinforced her determination to protect her kingdom and the ones she loves.

During her recovery, Elara starts to experience strange dreams. They are visions of her ancestors, the previous elemental sorceresses, who guide her and show her new ways to understand and harness her powers. With their guidance, Elara gradually recovers, her connection with the elements stronger than before.

Meanwhile, Darius is dealing with his own battle. He's torn between his responsibility as a prince and his lingering feelings for Elara. He tries to distance himself from her, focusing on bringing the perpetrators from his kingdom to justice. However, the more he tries to stay away, the more he finds himself drawn to her.

Unable to resist, Darius visits Elara. He apologizes for the betrayal from his kingdom and confesses his lingering feelings for her. He admits that he still loves her and is willing to fight for her, even if it means going against his own people.

This declaration stirs up old feelings in Elara. She's torn between her love for Alden and the strong connection she feels with

Darius. Alden, who witnesses this exchange, is heartbroken but hides his feelings, respecting Elara's confusion and giving her space to figure things out.

As Elara struggles with her feelings, Faelore comes under attack again. The rebel sorcerers from Faelore and the Dark Kingdom unite and launch an attack, aiming to dethrone the elemental sorceress and seize control over the kingdoms.

With the kingdom under attack, Elara, Alden, and Darius set their personal feelings aside and unite to protect Faelore.
As they fight off the invaders, their bonds are tested, and they find themselves battling not just for their kingdoms, but for love as well.

Chapter 20: The New Dawn

The united attack from the rebel sorcerers proves to be the most challenging test yet for Elara, Alden, and Darius. Despite the strength of their adversaries, the trio fights with all their might. Elara, fully embracing her power, leads the defense, with Alden and Darius by her side.

The battle is intense and fierce. Alden, showcasing his knightly skills, protects Elara from any harm while also keeping the attackers at bay. Darius, on the other hand, uses his knowledge of the Dark Kingdom's sorcery to counter the attackers, even as it pains him to fight his own kind.

Elara, tapping into her newly understood powers, controls her elements with an ease she has never felt before. She manages to hold off the attackers, gradually driving them back. After a long and arduous battle, they manage to defeat the rebel sorcerers, restoring peace and security to Faelore and the Dark Kingdom.

In the aftermath of the battle, Darius returns to his kingdom, carrying with him the heavy burden of betrayal and conflict. He takes it upon himself to root out the dissent in his kingdom and rebuild the trust that was lost.

Alden, despite his heartache, stays true to his promise. He continues to serve and protect Elara, even though it pains him to see her struggle with her feelings for Darius. His loyalty and love for Elara remain unwavering, reinforcing his position as her protector.

Elara, in the wake of the battle, finally makes peace with her powers. She embraces her role as a sorceress, realizing that her powers are a part of her identity, not a burden to be feared. Her decision about her love life, though, remains complex.

Elara takes a walk with Alden. She tells him that while she has feelings for Darius, she has chosen to be with Alden. She explains that her love for Alden is profound and unwavering, just like his love for her. Alden, overjoyed, holds Elara close, promising to always be by her side.

A new dawn rises over Faelore, bringing with it a renewed sense of hope and peace. Elara, finally at peace with her powers and her heart, looks forward to a new beginning with Alden by her side and her kingdom safe from threats. She has not only mastered her powers but also learned to balance her responsibilities as a sorceress and her desires as a woman in love. This journey, while arduous, has made her stronger and wiser, ready to face whatever comes next in her life.

Other Books In The Series:

Book 2
Elemental Soul: A Waltz of Duty and Desire

Book 3
Elemental Spirit: A Symphony of Destiny and Devotion